T0207875

THE OWNER
OF THE
CAROUSEL

L.G. RODRICKSON

BALBOA.PRESS
A DIVISION OF HAY HOUSE

The Gospel of Thomas:
Nag Hammadi library, Codex II, 2, pp. 32,10 to 51,28;
translated from the Coptic by Marvin Mayer

Balboa Press books may be ordered through booksellers or by contacting:

Balboa Press
A Division of Hay House
1663 Liberty Drive
Bloomington, IN 47403
www.balboapress.com
1 (877) 407-4847

Print information available on the last page.

ISBN: 978-1-9822-3617-5 (sc)
ISBN: 978-1-9822-3616-8 (e)

Balboa Press rev. date: 10/14/2019

"To my Family…and to those who seek
in their solitude: You are not alone."

Contents

PART I
Satori

Nothingness, existing in perfect ignorance of yourself is the most exotic ride, a divine drug that relieves the suffering caused by consciousness and unleashes from you that adventure called "existence." As you find yourself again arriving at the beginning, you remember it all and laugh aloud, realizing it was all a game, the result you get for inserting a coin on an old carousel machine. Later, *Solitude* welcomes you back from your ride, sits by your side, attentively listens your story, but reminds you at the end, that you have failed once again to capture something different than yourself while fishing in that endless ocean of desires. All that remains is the vanishing memory of this last merge, a universe I named "Joshuan." I remember its clear morning skies and the wind that was blessed everyday by a radiant artist making its eternal presentation in the natural blue cinema screen. For eons, I imagined that show, a spectacle of such magnificence even the waves of the seas didn't get tire of screaming at their sky idol, a parade tropical flamboyant trees couldn't resist to applaud with their seed pods. Another harmonious melody of fractal equations was this brief fantasy of mathematically simulated counterparts, one more drama among an infinite amount of plays, the positive and the negative actors dancing together again in the exquisite mind of a child. *Solitude*, listen carefully, this is how it began.

PART II
A Professional Autistic

All is perfect, everything flawless, except the psychiatrists' continuous obsession with my infinite imagination, and their constant questioning aimed to satisfy their insatiable quest for understanding. Yet here I am, once more, trading a splendorous encounter with Nature for the poor experience of meeting their unawareness. *"I wonder what is on your mind lonely child…if I only knew what imprisons your attention and causes your quietness…,"* a doctor with a noble and solitary life used to say to me, puzzled, calling my preference to respond in the language of silence, "autistic behavior." Convinced by his observations, he revealed the results of his diagnosis to my parents. He walked me out of his office, towards a cold waiting room where my father and my mother awaited, with frustration, an explanation for my perceived unresponsiveness, my long empty stares at the walls, and my ability to distract myself, for hours, watching drops of water fall from a leaking faucet. He closed the door, sat on his chair and said, "your son Joshuan has a condition known as Autism. We have no explanation or a cure for what causes his behavior. Children like your son are special. Sometimes they develop extraordinary abilities. Who knows, perhaps in the future, with the application of behavioral therapies, medications and some patience, your son could become a functional and ordinary human being, maybe a savant…a master mathematician."

I was four years of age then; the cause of my Autism was still a mystery to the greatest human minds. According to the psychiatrist, my chances of development as an "ordinary human being," fully awakened, functional and responsive to love, affection, and society, were small. I had no significant speech. My greatest talent was, however, *to clearly perceive the secret feelings in the hearts of people.* Being ridiculed occasionally was tolerable, but seeing my parents depart from me soon after they heard my diagnosis, was deeply shattering. Perhaps, they abandoned me because of my inability to gaze at their eyes and express, with words, the feelings I had, my appreciation for their care. They never accepted my uniqueness and never discovered that I was just an old passerby disguised in the body of a child. One who had chosen to help people with special needs, people who for a strange reason called themselves "normal," sailing on their every-day-ships to nowhere, without a Polaris on their firmaments. To those I, and other colleagues devote our services in this orphanage we call home. And now, three years later, I am here, sitting again in this carousel, enjoying the ride, realizing a plan for the day in the form of thoughts that appear from nowhere: "Joshuan, it's time for your session with Sophia, the behavioral therapist."

Helping people like Sophia was not an easy task. Sophia was one of my toughest patients, one who had tasted the bitter part of her life since she was a child. Her parents died on a terrorist attack when she was five years of age. Just like me, she lived in an orphanage for years without enjoying the care of a family. After being married for three years, her inability to conceive children sparked a series of events that ended on a divorce. I knew her well. I could perceive her many misfortunes and her life full of deceptions in every behavioral therapy session. Like many people in this world, bombarded by the nuclear war of their lives, Sophia was surviving her sorrow in her aloneness, but her smile was always present when she had to pretend that she was emotionally stable. A professionally accomplished woman though, she could not disguise from me her need for love and the kindness of a helping hand. She was now entering that stage in human existence where the mind has no other choice but to make a pause, questioning the rationale and the purpose of it all, balancing an act of sanity along the narrow path of a rope, the place where fragrant flowers easily lose their contest against the pleasing smoke of a cigarette, where a drug offers flash forgiveness and the evanescent illusion of disappearing. Despite her circumstances, she still prayed during the nights, with her hope the size of planets, and her virgin-unused faith, the seed I was intending to finally help her sow. After weeks of therapy sessions, I was passionately determined to finally help cure her condition. As a professional autistic, I knew exactly what I had to do. Sophia entered the therapy room, as usual, her body present, but absent minded, deeply wandering in the world of her grief. When she greeted me, I pretend I didn't hear her, showing no attention, giving no reply. When she tried to make eye contact with me, I completely ignored her presence. When she gave me the toys to perform the "therapy-of-the-day," I simply refused to cooperate. Everything was going per the plan; Sophia was now losing her patience. This was particularly difficult because she had been trained in academia to deal with my *autistic talents*. The more she tried to work with me, the more distressed and unpleased I appeared. After a while, I realized my traditional autistic techniques were not being effective enough. I decided to use my "melt-down," my ultimate therapy method of last resource. I threw myself on the floor, violently moving my head from side to side. With my arms and legs shaking, I started crying and screaming as loud as I could, just like a professional autistic knows how to do well. It worked; Sophia completely lost her composure. She sat on her chair, exhausted, slowly massaging her face with the palms of her hands, almost about to cry. "Could this be finally success? Could this be finally the day of her awakening?" I wondered, just waiting for a confirmation, the words that were just about to come from her deepest feelings. A few seconds passed…and then she said, "This life of mine is not working at all…I need to do something different…I need to change…. Joshuan, I care immensely for you, but I need some time off to put myself together."

My mission with Sophia seemed accomplished. A mystery of mysteries was the fact that she always thought that I was the one who needed therapy. The second stage of this treatment was now on its way, in flawless synchronicity with the wonders of Earth. Sophia decided to take a vacation in a wild environment, where Nature was waiting for her to continue the therapy session I had initiated miles away. Mesmerized by her silent conversation with trees, flowers, and waterfalls, she received a full dose of motivation and hope. Her experience, all in an encounter with herself, made her re-think about her lost Polaris, something the everyday news, traffic jams, busy work schedules, and a world in ceaseless conflict never allows people to do. Nature is the supreme psychologist, no human genius surpasses her expertise, her wisdom, and motherhood. Whether we demand for it or not, change always makes its impersonal appearance in our lives, signaling our preparedness for a different carousel ride. On her trip back home, Sophia met her counterpart, a good man with a loving heart who was also living an empty and solitary existence. After sharing their experiences and living together for some time, they decided to formally join their lives. She had now access to taste the sweet part of her human experience. I was joyful to see her smile during our new therapy sessions, and was proud to know I had been, in my own silent way, a secret contributor to her new way of living. She had been one of several people I had treated successfully using my autistic techniques, such as those who had also found the meaning of their lives in the most unusual way, sharing some of their precious time with divine beings disguised as vagabonds, animals, or people labeled by society as "disabled." As for me, a seven-year-old child with special talents no family desired, I always felt unwelcomed in this perpetual Halloween, where only a few know they are disguised, and most are sleep-walking their lives. I wondered if I still had a chance to find a new family, a new home. Just like Sophia, I found myself speaking to the Owner of the Carousel during the nights, searching for clues in the realms of my dreams: *"Oh, great architect of dramas and games…I know you purposely scripted my role in this way. I genuinely desire to act in your play, to enjoy your imaginative adventures with grace. If there is still a possibility for me to experience the love of a family in this ride, please, let my body express at least a bit of the love I am capable of sharing, so people are not disappointed of me, and may choose to discard me as my father and my mother did."*

A few weeks passed, and I was getting anxious, realizing I had lost my talent of *perceiving the hidden feelings in the hearts of people*, as I always could. Worst, no new patients had come to visit me in the therapy room, searching for my professional autistic services. Long became my days inside the walls of the orphanage, and long were also the days for my colleagues with Down syndrome and others with special talents families also disliked. We were together enduring the pain caused by the cruel mistreatment and the indifference of those who consider themselves ''normal,'' and don't realize we have a purpose and a role to play in this world. When the Owner of the Carousel reverses the ride, where would they hide? Evidently, they ignore they could be the mothers and fathers of those who will be putting-on our shoes tomorrow. One morning, Sophia returned to the orphanage, not to work, but to resign to her duties as a behavioral therapist. Her face was still glowing with joy, and so was by her side, Oliver, the good man who was now her husband. After farewelling the other children, she asked to meet me in the therapy room. She was no longer in need of my services anymore. This was, perhaps, the last moment in the crossing of our paths, our last opportunity to see each other. After gazing at me with utmost compassion, she grabbed my hands and said the most extraordinary words I had ever heard: "Joshuan, would you like to be our son?" All the hairs on my skin stud up waiting for my response. I felt immersed in my feelings. I wanted to hug them and tell them that those words had made me the happiest child in the entire creation, but my autistic talents prevented my body, my speech, from expressing my emotions. *"I wonder what is on your mind lonely child…?"* said Oliver, *the psychiatrist who used to be solitary,* putting his hands over her shoulders, never expecting my reply. Suddenly, I felt a great power surrounded my entire body. I immediately realized it was the invisible presence of the Owner of the Carousel, answering my desires. In an instant, that power transformed me in a way I could not understand, but I was now free, and in full control of myself. The sensations, the feelings were too powerful to contain. My emotions materialized into tears, as

I gazed deeply into their eyes and express, in the language of the world, for the first time, what had been imprisoned in me for years. No longer was this the case. The words inevitably came out: "I would love to be your son."

PART III
An Ordinary Human Being

> *"And he said, Humankind is like a wise fisherman, who cast his net into the sea and drew it up from the sea full of little fish. Among the fish, he found a fine large fish. He threw all the little fish back into the sea and easily chose the large fish."*
>
> - The Gospel of Thomas

"Sophia, Oliver, here we meet again, another cloudy and windy afternoon, just like that strange day I lost consciousness and felt into a deep sleep on a shore. Contrary to what my friends said that day, I did see and spoke to that man... it wasn't a dream. I sat next to him on the sand and saw his smile and the tears on his face. It was not a hallucination. Only you Sophia, only you believed my story. You knew I was telling a truth. This was one of several testimonies of your wisdom and love. But now, that's all part of the past. Twenty-one summers have come and gone since both of you were transformed into a nightmare by that tragic car accident you experienced. Oliver, Sophia, I will never forget your gift of supreme love and compassion, the one people believed cured my autism and erased those mysterious memories of my childhood. Coming to this tomb is no longer necessary. I know you are no longer here. But, where have you gone? You have left me on this orphanage people call 'Earth,' under the attention of this invisible caregiver, this god of silence that always hides above the firmament and depends on holy books, priests, and monks to communicate his will. A god that gives you a left hand but takes the right, provides you a banquette when you are not hungry, a desert when you are thirsty, and never provides clear and direct answers to not even the simplest of my philosophical questions. You god of nothingness…you are as necessary as this tomb. Come here now and show up your face, you senseless coward. Where are you hiding Oliver, Sophia, and all of those who have departed this world? Come and explain to us the purpose of this pointless creation of yours. Don't try to entertain me like a child with your beautiful blue skies, your night stars, your oceans and your forests. Pause this carousel of shit now, and tell us what we are, the reason behind this brutal game of survival and change you like us to play so much." The silence of this god is too painful. He doesn't even accept my offer to return his "gift of freewill." This must be his hell, and survival and change…the fuel of its fire. So much hunger, war, hate, and confusion…. All that we have is each other, our sorrow and our happiness, the consequences of our love and madness, our utopian hopes and our dreams, these vehicles of water and dust, and the noise of our ignorance. "I'm not done yet with you and your silence you god of misery; I will keep on searching until I find the truth. If I had the chance to put on your shoes, I would be a better god than you, one with only eternal bliss, goodness and joy, without senseless rules and irrational salvation plans. Until that day comes, I will play your game. I will continue to be the Math professor in that old university. Thru Math, Science, and rationality, I will be able to understand your craziness, and the mystery of your silence."

"Young man…Math, Science, and rationality

have never been enough," said an old woman who was, for my embarrassment, listening my conversation with the wind.

"That terrible god of yours is closer to you than you think, so close, you don't even recognize its presence. Some abductive reasoning may be appropriate for you at this point in your existence, that which ignorant fanatics call "the mystical, the occult." You would be surprised to know that the rationality of Science and Math, which you have already tasted, is the missing cornerstone of the so-called 'mystics.' When you make of both one, then you will be able to realize the truth you are so obsessively trying to find."

"Lady, you don't know…nor can you understand what I am searching for," I replied to her, annoyed by the impertinence of her words.

"The cards will…if you can overcome your arrogance and your fear, the cards will reveal your destiny, your truth," she said, extending her hand to provide, in a small piece of paper, her physical address.

"Lady, it is because of this nonsense people like you offer that this world is so full of ignorance and agony. Only thru sound reasoning and critical thinking can a human being understand himself and the world he lives in. You and those like you have been able to explain nothing about this universe," I replied to her, indifferent about her feelings or her reaction.

"Young man, you have never paused to think that the god you judge with such severity may be an ordinary human being like you, incapable of understanding his true nature, a dreamer eternally surviving loneliness, like an orphan child without the love of a family, without friends and toys to play, only with the companionship of his own imagination, the size of a universe. When you are ready, it will be your turn; then, I will be honored to become a character in your story, and a first-hand-witness to a new beginning. Until that moment arrives, don't suffer trying to understand how this carousel works…just enjoy the ride. Remember, when you are ready, the cards will tell…." After saying these words, she gently grabbed my hand and placed the small piece of paper on my palm, and then she walked away into the woods, leaving me in the company of an empty tomb, the rain, and the wind.

PART IV
A Master
Mathematician

> *"…Seek and do not stop seeking until you find. When you find, you will be disturbed. When you are disturbed, you will marvel and rule over all."*
>
> - The Gospel of Thomas

"Are you ready? It is now your turn," gently said the fortuneteller as she opened the door to her cabin in the middle of the wilderness. Everybody in the world seemed gone that night; all except the full moon, my hidden fears, and the strange old woman who was about to "reveal" my destiny, my truth. I followed her to a very dark room, where my sense of smell was welcomed by a strong scent of incense. Waiting in full darkness, I was expecting her to turn-on the lights, but she never did. I could hear her steps in the dark, the door closing behind me, and could feel the gentle breeze of air displaced by her walk across the room. Although I've never been afraid of the occult, I must confess my experience was now turning a bit intense. I then saw the shimmering light of a small candle

on the top of a table; Tarot cards were next to it. I wondered if the light of the candle would be enough for her to see the images on the cards with clarity; she looked at me and said, "Yes; you may sit now." Every hair on my skin erupted violently, reminding me I was alive and not hallucinating. "Is this woman reading my mind?" I questioned myself, almost convinced I had to leave. With hesitation, I sat in front of her, not knowing how to react. She never stopped staring at me, not even blinking for a second, slowly, very slowly shuffling the cards from one hand to the other. I knew well she had discovered my fear. But how could I have prevented my eyes from revealing my feelings, undoubtedly an impossible task, only a reality in a world where infants purposely disguise their innocence. My awareness seemed long gone, a fraction of a second from almost being hypnotized, transformed by her eyes and the timeless movement of her hands. A moment face-to-face with infinity this seemed to be, and then she woke me up with a mundane instruction: "Take three cards; the cards you pick will provide the message your heart needs to know." I picked the cards and turned them on the table, displaying their colorful but odd images. She looked at the cards and then she closed her eyes. The room was entirely silent. Then, she said with her graceful voice, *"your imagination will create the world of your future...*you may go now."

I felt like a sailor who receives a misunderstood instruction from his captain in the middle of a raging storm in a deep ocean. Without doubt, my alertness was back, and so was, my lack of understanding. "All of that waiting, the senseless drama, to hear such an unreasonable and simplistic statement," I thought. I was hoping she would predict my future or reveal details regarding the purpose of the rare events that had occurred during my alleged and now forgotten autistic childhood. At least it was a good thing she refused to get paid for her service. Nevertheless, my feelings were trying to make me believe her simple words had an important meaning. Maybe her message was predicting that my mathematical equations were close to bringing the long-awaited answers to my research, that my work as a mathematician would help create the "world of the future." How adventurous is this ignorance I carry. Only in the clownish fantasies of my imagination could such interpretation be considered a reality. There is no space in my life for this absurd mysticism. "If only my colleagues knew where I am, what I'm doing here…" I reasoned, concerned about my reputation as a man of academia, walking out of her cabin confused and disappointed.

My drive back home that night seemed like an endless trip thru uncertainty. The words of the fortuneteller were as puzzling as those I heard from that strange man, during that inexplicable incident on the beach. Despite of all these years, I still have a clear memory of that cloudy and windy afternoon. I was the happiest child alive, building cities on the sand, enjoying the wonders of the seashore with my friends. Every living experience during those childhood years felt like a treasure to be uncovered, an adventure granted by the kindness and compassionate love of Oliver and Sophia. My friends and I were alone on the beach that day, just blocks away from our homes.

As I looked far away along the curved shore, there was a man sitting on the sand, completely by himself. For two long hours, as my friends and I played, I noticed the man did nothing but stare at the sea. For a strange reason, I felt the deepest compassion for him, and wondered what was the reason for his aloneness. "Maybe he wants to play with us; he wants to join us, but he is too afraid to ask," I thought with my childish innocence. I felt a need to approach him, surrendering to the intense magnet of my curiosity. Walking towards him, leaving my friends behind me as they ignored my departure, I started looking at the sea, trying to find the cause of the man's distraction far in the horizon; but nothing was there, except the eternal marriage between the sky and the ocean. When I finally reached him, he came out of his posture, and received me with a smile although tears appeared fresh on his cheeks. His smile, however, made me feel entirely at ease, like a typical encounter with a family member I knew very well. I was about to ask if he wanted to play with us, but for some reason I just asked, "Who are you?" I was expecting to hear his name as a reply, but instead, he asked me to sit next to him, and spoke to me words, a short story I could not understand. Soon after his last word had been spoken, I felt into a deep sleep. After some hours, my friends and Sophia said they had found me laying on the sand, alone. When I told my story to everyone, the reason I had been lost, nobody believed me and thought I was hallucinating. Doctors speculated that I was suffering of some form of psychosis. Others thought traces of autism were still in me. Thus, I went into a state of depression. It was Sophia, again, in which I found support and an anchor to reality, to knowledge and reason. She was the only one who believed my story was true. Many years have passed, but I still can remember every one of the man's words, full of mystery; but their meaning has been hidden by my ignorance.

Leaving the fortuneteller session behind me, I woke up the next morning, ready for a new day of work at the university. When I arrived at my desk, pleased with the unmatched aroma of my everyday morning cup of tea on hand, I started reviewing my mathematical equations, with a pursuit of glory that only passionate treasure hunters are capable of understanding. But all my efforts were in vane; the pinnacle of my success seemed as near as the Andromeda galaxy. My meeting with failure was then abruptly interrupted by a conversation I heard between two colleagues who were next door:

"No good results yet? You should change your approach and move in a different direction; you should consider other possibilities, something out of the ordinary may change your perspective. Go take a break, read a book, refresh your mind."

Although these words were not spoken directly to me, I made them mine; they certainly made sense. After spending long years, trying to solve what many of my colleagues considered "impossible," at least I could break the prison of my office for one hour. Like a dancer eager to arrive to his weekend celebration, I went to a bookstore. I desperately started searching for my afternoon tea at the shop, and later, the Math and

Science book sections. Browsing between walls of books, I saw a very old woman on a wheel chair, with huge spectacles, long hair, and a smile that revealed she was not having a good day. "Why would a publisher want to sell a book with empty pages, and still pretend readers will pay for it?" she groaned at me, rising and shaking a book with her right hand. Obviously upset, she put the book back on the shelf and left without noticing the book ended on the floor. Surprised to see her loud show had caught nobody's attention but mine, I leaned to rescue the book from the floor, and I noticed it had no title. Even more surprising was the fact that the book wasn't empty, it had scripts all over its pages. "That poor old lady must be blind," I thought, as I discovered -to my disappointment- that it was some sort of manuscript showing alchemical symbols describing mystical and occult practices. When I almost had decided to disregard the manuscript as the work of charlatanism, the words of that conversation I heard at the university rushed-in to "save" the manuscript: "Maybe you should consider other possibilities, something out of the ordinary...." After a while, I sat on a chair and started glancing over some of its pages. After all, the idea was to take a break, to divert my attention from the complex Fractal mathematical problems I was so obsessively trying to solve. Curiously, I recognized the author of the manuscript had the same name of a prominent scholar I knew about, a mathematician whose work had been recognized by historical textbooks. Soon after publishing his work, he suddenly and mysteriously disappeared from public appearances. No one knew where he was. Perhaps, what he thought as being relevant conclusions were so extravagant and mistaken, he may have been rejected and ridiculed by the academic community. His disappearance was as intriguing as the subject of what appeared to be a manuscript written by his own hand. But, if this is legitimate, why would a rational intellectual write a series of essays about alchemical practices and mysticism? One of the observations written on the manuscript read: "A key to understanding the profound secrets of creation can be found by mastering imagination...." By now, trying to forget the memory of that fortuneteller session was even more difficult than solving my mathematical equations. Why fear the contents of a book? A need to satisfy my nosiness finally convinced me to make the ridiculous decision of buying the manuscript. Throughout my life, I had suppressed any interest in reading books about religion, mysticism or the occult, but the fact that the manuscript in front of me had been allegedly written by the objective mind of a mathematician like myself, made it interesting. I returned to the university, finished my work tasks, and immediately went back home. In a rare way, I was excited to continue my reading experience with the manuscript. A short time of mild distraction later transformed into adventure and fascination. I even decided to take a few days off work to allow me the time to read without interruptions. I was so engaged with the writings of the manuscript, I read day and night, only stopping when I was tired, hungry, or in need of a nap. At last, a bear had his chance to enjoy his first meal after a long period of hibernation. After seven days, I reached the final words of the manuscript: "*Endless fractal patterning…the snake that bites its own tail.*" I found myself in a two-way path. Choosing not to believe the statements written on the manuscript, and keeping my objective mind intact, meant an easy escape to my every-day-world. However, pretending my sudden awakening of consciousness was just the result of silly dreams, or self-delusions, was not the option my heart was willing to accept. I was almost convinced the words of the manuscript possessed a truth, a key that could guide me to understand the fractal reality of life, which was implicit in my math equations. "Should I continue with this...?" I inquired myself, as thoughts started cascading into the pond of my mind:

"Could that I have been conditioned to believe as truth, be mistaken?"

"Could the purpose of life be much more than just surviving, suffering, being happy, or having failure or success?"

"A key to understanding the profound secrets of creation can be found by mastering imagination...."

"Maybe you should consider other possibilities, something out of the ordinary…."

"If I choose to continue my way of existence, I know what to expect; but if I choose to experience the unknown, what could happen?"

Powerless against the force of my curiosity, I made the decision to seriously explore the promises of the manuscript in my aloneness; I started practicing its exercises. Ironically, the first exercise I had to master required doing absolutely nothing, to experience the presence of *Silence*. After several hours, days, and months of relentless practice, I finally could reach it one night. It had startling things to offer, but *Ego* had always kept it occulted. Once *Ego* noticed my persistence to pay exclusive attention to *Silence*, it had no other choice but to retreat. Now, *Silence* was here, bringing me tranquility like I never had felt before. Its presence reminded me: "Zero is the origin of all…."

Whether I was prepared or not, *Silence* was revealing to me, in a place of complete emptiness, with a simple thought, a mystery, a reflection with profound implications I often had taken for granted. During my years of math research, I always found great excitement, entertainment, and distraction working with complicated numbers and patterns, but I never paused to think about their origins. I was marveled by the simplicity and elegance of this revelation. Then, from nowhere, in a fraction of a second, *Ego* made its return. It was anxious to know about my encounter with *Silence*. "What did *Silence* make you believe?" *Ego* asked emphatically. "Whatever you may have realized from being in its presence should not be taken seriously; I am The One." For a moment, I noticed *Ego's* reaction was more like that of an entity who was fearful, more than it resembled a character of power or authority. For a strange reason, *Ego* could not withstand *Silence*. Its presence provoked me to ask, "Who are you?" The answer came as quick as lightning, "I am Joshuan, the greatest mathematician the world has ever seen. I am the negative and positive values above and below Zero." I then asked *Ego*, "What is your origin? How did you come into existence?" Like trying to remember the memories of an extremely remote past, a short encounter with eternity, and its reply came with a voice that resembled some sort of nostalgia: "My origin is *Silence...*my driver: spontaneous curiosity and desire." Just like *Silence*, *Ego* had its own profound mysteries to reveal. But just when I wanted to explore further into the realms of my consciousness, I found myself awakened, surrounded by the world that was always there, well known by my senses, waiting for me at the end of every meditation session.

For many years, after returning from work, I continually practiced the exercises of the manuscript; first, mastering the art of meditation, and later, experimenting with creative visualizations. Because I wanted to have good records of my practices, I wrote detailed notes about my progress with all my mystical experiences. I had written my own notes all over the pages of the manuscript. The whole experience was like keeping a diary of my life. Persistence was a key to my perceived transformation. As I practiced, my meditation and visualization experiences became more and more intense. I rediscovered I could unlimitedly create whatever I wanted with my imagination, like playing being the god of my own world. My intimate sessions with *Silence* and *Ego* were expanding my self-knowledge far beyond my preconceived beliefs and ideas. A single molecule of water was now starting to understand the ocean and its own natural cycles. Caught between reason and illusion, my mystical sessions were, in occasions, so vivid, I couldn't tell if I was having a real-world experience, or if it was just the result of my own imaginative mind. Strangely, in the universe of my imagination, the things I had created: people of all ages, races and genders, animals, plants, locations... all considered me to be their "creator," but for a reason I couldn't perceive, they were incapable of clearly understanding my nature, nor the purpose driving my practices. I was considered, in fact, their greatest unresolved mystery. Every time I wanted to expand my mystical experience beyond this point, I suddenly woke up in the "real" world. It was like facing a wall, which I had the impression I wasn't allowed or ready to trespass.

In my world of lectures, tea, and equations, patience and detachment were at last delivering its rewards; my math work had received the full recognition of my colleagues, and the attention of prestigious universities and governments around the world. I was being nominated for important academic achievement awards as my work was being discussed all over the globe. It seemed, the solutions to the problems that once evaded my reasoning, were now flowing limitlessly in my mind, without any disruptions or impediments. Advancements in Artificial Intelligence were now being realized based on my mathematical discoveries. I felt professionally accomplished, but miserably tired by the shadow of my academic success. Yet, in the mysterious and secret world of my introverted occult practices, there was one event still unaccomplished: I wanted to explore what was beyond that wall that prevented me from fully "living and merging" with my imaginative creations.

One night, immersed in my solitude, driven by pure curiosity and desire, I plunged into the deepest state of meditation, and was immediately embraced by *Silence.* As it was typical, only after achieving the greatest nothingness *Silence* could offer, beyond the usual feelings of vibrations, the impossibly beautiful patterns of lights and sound frequencies, I started visualizing and recreating, with detail, the world I had in my imagination. Then, I was confronted with the "wall." Thoughts from memories came to my mind: "If I choose to continue my way of existence, I know what to expect; but if I choose to experience the unknown, what could happen?" This was the moment in which the missing cornerstone, a great secret, was at last exposed to me: *the "wall" was the representation of my fear of the unknown.* As a result of this breakthrough, the wall suddenly vanished. There was no turning back now. I felt ready and willing to move forward; I made the decision and took the step to go beyond the grandiose veil of beautiful psychedelic geometries and colors. And then, I instantly found myself *totally awakened* in the world of my own creation...a face-to-face meeting with my newborn child, result of my passionate affair with my beloved imagination. The feeling…overwhelming ecstasy…like a lover entering a bridal chamber to receive the true love of his dreams for the first time. Everything was there, the fragrance of the flowers, the beauty of the mountains, the sweetness of the fruits, the smooth welcoming touch and sound of the wind. All I had imagined and visualized during the many years of my devoted practice was now here, a reality I could vividly and consciously experience, limitlessly, with all my senses. However, with the thrill of this powerful experience also came an extraordinary realization that disturbed me: *I had now become the "Creator" of my own world; and at the same time, another famous mathematician who had mysteriously disappeared.* My secret practices, all meticulously annotated on the pages of the manuscript were now considered by some academics as *"the proof of the genius's insanity;"* and *"a new holy book"* by religious fanatics who were desperately trying to explain the birth of their universe and its creator. But this moment of awe was suddenly transformed into the deepest sadness when I discovered the creatures of my new creation were unsatisfied and suffering. Unable to realize the purpose of their existence, they questioned the origins of their reality with hard judgment, fear, and even hate, waging conflicts and destroying all I had created with the greatest care, passion, and devotion. Not even my constant presence in the forms of infinite blue skies, clear nights full of stars, the vastness of the oceans, or the richness of the forests could provide enough happiness, comfort, or reveal the clues to the loving nature of their existence and freewill.

Dishearten and confounded by feelings of disillusionment, I took rest on a shoreline, gazing at a horizon, with the purest sense of loneliness in me, wondering what had gone wrong. Evidently, the cruelty and brutality of the evilness and ignorance deeply concealed behind my love and wisdom, managed to manifest itself as the shadow of my benevolence. How could I have prevented this suffering and chaos from happening? Goodness alone cannot exist without evilness;

both need each other to exist in a relative drama of counterparts. I felt overwhelmed by my new reality. My workings were only appreciated by the adventurous souls of the children, who seemed to be the only ones truly pleased with the wonders of my creation, gracefully enjoying my carousel without asking how it came to be. They became my consolation, the inspiration giving meaning to my existence, and the root of my fractal creations. To them I awarded my kingdom. One, with particular curiosity, sat by my side, asking me, *"Who are you?"* The greatness of his innocence made him more than prepared to receive an answer: *"When I was All, immersed in my solitude, driven by pure curiosity and desire, I decided to journey, to merge with my imagination. Spellbound, and greatly in love with my imagination, I forgot who I was as my beloved creation was born. Now, fully awakened, as an old carousel ride transforms into a memory, I have realized again, what I am.*

Printed in the United States
By Bookmasters